KARL EL-KOURA

The Lost Stories

A Series of Cosmic Adventures

Publication History

"Lost Eternity," "Lost Inheritance," "Lost Time," "Lost Word," "Lost Ship," "Lost Opportunity," and "Lost Reward" were first published in *GateWay S-F Magazine* from 2001 to 2006.

The author is grateful to the editors of GateWay S-F *for their support and encouragement, especially B. Joseph Fekete, Jr., John A.M. Darnell, and Lawrence Green.*

To my amo Saad

Contents

Introduction

"FEGHOOTS" is the name given to a certain kind of story: usually a bit silly, often contrived, always ending in a groan-inducing pun. In bad cases, a feghoot isn't a story but a joke; in better cases, a feghoot is an interesting story in its own right, with the pun-ending adding a layer of detective story, where instead of figuring out whodunit, the reader tries to anticipate the final line.

I didn't know any of that when I wrote "Lost Eternity," the first story in this collection. It was 1994, I was 15 years old, and I'd decided I wanted to write for a living. Although young, I was smart enough to know the steps I needed to go through to achieve my goal. Step 1: write a story. Step 2: get it published. Step 3: don't lose your head when you become rich and famous. To tackle Step 1, I thought of one of my favorite authors at the time, Isaac Asimov, and some of his stories, especially the ones that ended in puns. Those were clever, funny, and—best of all—very short. The latter quality appealed to me on two levels: first, I figured a magazine would be more likely to take a chance on an unknown author when the story was a short-short, and, second, with perhaps a bit of laziness tempering my ambition, I felt it would be easier to write a shorter story than a longer one. That summer I assigned my mind the task of thinking up a good story and a good pun. Why I picked a religious pun, I'm not sure. I was born into a Christian family and have been a lifelong believer, but it would only be a few years later that I really embraced my spiritual side and faith became a powerful force in my life.

Step 2. I don't remember how long I deliberated on where I wanted my first story to be published. I settled on *The Magazine of Fantasy and Science Fiction*, the top speculative fiction magazine at the time and, unbeknownst to me, the magazine that had originally published Richard Bretnor's Ferdinand Feghoot stories (the ones that give this type of story its name).

I heard from *The Magazine of Fantasy and Science Fiction* at the end of the summer. Strangely, bewilderingly, amazingly, they didn't want to publish my little story (so much for Step 2, let alone Step 3). But school was starting up again and there were assignments to complete, exams to study for, sports to play, and girls to figure out (not necessarily in that order), and I decided to go back to Step 1 when I had a bit of free time (the idea that one could send a story rejected by one professional magazine to another professional magazine, an obvious and universal practice among writers, took me a few years to figure out). When my brother, who is two years my senior, was looking for work to publish in our high school's poetry and short story anthology, which he and his friends were editing, I submitted "Lost Eternity."

That publication led to one of the greatest writing memories I have. My uncle Saad, who was attending university in Alabama, came to visit us in Ottawa, Ontario during the summer of 1995. The anthology was on the shelf in our computer room and when my uncle found out I had a story in it, he wanted to read my work. I remember standing beside him while he read the story, stopping every once in a while to laugh out loud or to tell me he liked a particular line. Although it was more than a decade and a half ago, I can remember exactly which parts made him laugh: the mix of colors that made up the plain-yellow bush, the words "Gamma Bamma," the pun at the end. Perhaps this is the kind of early encouragement any artist needs to keep pursuing and trying to perfect their craft. For me, from someone I really admired (my uncle was the personification of cool, as far as I was concerned), that reaction was priceless. This book is dedicated to the memory of my amo Saad, "amo" being the Arabic word for uncle. In December of that same year, he and some friends were driving home in bad weather and the driver lost control of the car, which swerved off the road and crashed into a tree. The tree collapsed onto my uncle, who was napping in the back seat, and killed him instantly. I have many cherished memories of my uncle, but watching him read through my story, enjoy it (or at least fake it really well), and then laugh out loud when he came to the end is a particularly special and meaningful one.

I liked "Lost Eternity" and, although you only see glimpses of him in that first story, I liked the main character. Years later, a man named B. Joseph Fekete was editing a magazine of Christian speculative fiction called *GateWay S-F*. I'd sold Joe a few original stories, and one day I remembered "Lost Eternity." I sent it to him to see if he'd be interested in publishing it. He was interested, and he and his assistant editor asked if I, in turn, would be interested in turning the story into a series.

Over the course of the next five years, Joe published six more "Lost" stories, the writing of which was often instigated by Joe sending me friendly emails wondering when he could expect the next installment.

We discussed putting together a chapbook once I'd felt I could wrap up the series, but unfortunately, in 2006, circumstances caused Joe to shut down the magazine and withdraw from his publishing work before that could happen.

Here is the complete series, from the first story that made my uncle laugh, to the ones Joe thankfully hassled me to write, to the final arc that, I hope you'll agree, take the series from silly but fun into territory a little more serious. That's the danger with God: you introduce Him as a minor character to help you sell a joke, and soon you realize He's taken over the whole show.

Karl El-Koura
August 2011
Ottawa, Ontario (Canada)

One

Lost Eternity

$\mathbf{M}$Y name is James Kollins, and I am captain of the galactic warship *DeVille*. This morning I received a top-priority message from Earth ordering me to take my ship to Eden and destroy its one and only colony. The Planopsychologists had rated Eden high in the Grumbles-Against-Earth category, which meant that if a rebellion was not imminent, it was at least somewhat possible.

Many of our technological secrets, some related to the Board of Terrestrial Defense and Offense, were in the heads and computers of these settlers. If the Other Side were to get their hands on those secrets, their technology would rival ours and then there'd be no end to this war. That was justification enough for me to cut my vacation short and jump to Eden. But I couldn't cut short the vacations of my crew; better captains than I have thrown away their lives in futile attempts to force their crew back to work before their shore leave was up.

Not that it mattered, as I took the *DeVille* to Eden and

made short work of the fifteen hundred or so settlers, destroying their colony in the better half of an hour. Not bad, considering I was not only flying solo but also trying to follow my favorite holodrama, *Captain Courageous and the Women Who Love Him.* The colonists took a few shots at my ship—repairing the damage they caused made me miss the last ten minutes of this week's *Captain Courageous*, for which trouble I wish damnation on their souls.

Though certain I had killed them all, orders are orders, so I proceeded to scan the planet centimeter-by-measly-centimeter. In an unexplored section on the east side of the planet, I picked up strange energy readings.

Landing my ship some two kilometers from the readings, I trekked by foot until I came to their origin—a huge, green and blue (with dashes of red here and there) yellow bush.

The bush emitted high frequencies of Gamma Bamma radiation, from which I deduced that it was recently hit by a sub-photonic laser—which could also explain why I saw nothing out of the ordinary (as far as bushes go) using only my eyes.

Being the personification of bravery I am reputed to be, and in defiance of the radiation that would scare away lesser men, I strode up to the bush and fearlessly touched it. As soon as I made contact, I heard a voice in my head. I pulled my hand away quickly and cut it off before the storm of words could overwhelm me.

After regaining my wits, I touched it again—but slower this time.

The same voice spoke to me. It hardly made any sense and I had to labor to understand, but by slow degrees I was able to begin making sense of the downpour of words.

To sum it up, the voice said it was called Lord and that, if I left the garden and then the planet, and promised that no other human being would set foot on its world ever again, it would grant me eternal life.

Which was great, except it wouldn't let go of me: both my hands were now touching the bush, and try as I might, I couldn't wrench them free.

"Before leave, about self, tell me," I finally made out.

Poor lonely guy, I thought, and started to recount my trials and tribulations through this life, my joys and my failures. I began with my childhood, and worked up from there, sometimes having to repeat myself twice or even three times before Lord could get things straight. I didn't mind; I figured it was good practice for writing my memoirs.

When I was finally finished, Lord said, "Interesting is this. Cannot give eternal life, though."

I was stupefied. I'm as modest as you'd like, but I know who I am, and nothing in all my recounting served to put me in a bad light.

"Lord!" I said, heating up. "We had a deal. I'll leave this planet, and I'll do my damnedest to make sure you're left alone. So explain to me why you won't keep your end of the bargain!"

There was a momentary pause before Lord replied, "My hands are tied. You warship the *DeVille*!"

Two

Lost Inheritance

CAPTAIN Courageous was giving his patented suggestive smile to a beautiful, scantily-clad, green-skinned alien when my ready room doors beeped.

Without any effort to hide my irritation, I said, "Yes? What is it?"

The doors split apart to reveal my second-in-command, Winston.

"Captain, I—" he began, then saw what was on the holo. "Oh, I didn't realize . . . I'm sorry to disturb you, sir."

I nodded for him to go on with a gracious smile, but made a mental note. If he couldn't remember when *Captain Courageous* was on, he wasn't the kind of officer I wanted serving under me.

"First things first," he said. "Your request to have the *DeVille* rechristened has been denied."

"What!" I said, coming out of my chair. "What's wrong with the *Ilovelord*—that's a fine name for a ship!"

Winston shrugged. "Second, we've been ordered to the Planet Meekton."

He handed me a report, but instead of reading it, I said, "Oh?"

"They've scored a 9.5 on the gee-ah-vee scale."

In my entire career, I'd never heard such a high Grumbles-Against-Earth rating.

"What's their grumble?" I said, glancing at the report.

"Something about getting what's theirs. The Board of Terrestrial Defense and Offense is keeping them from their so-called inheritance."

"We're to take them out?"

"Not according to orders," Winston said. "We're just supposed to scare them a little."

I put the report down and surveyed my first officer. "You've set a course already, haven't you?"

Winston nodded.

I turned and looked out the window. There was a large, mostly purplish planet spinning in space.

"That's Meekton, isn't it?"

My second-in-command nodded.

"Their Prime Minister or President or whoever's in charge is waiting to talk to me, aren't they?"

Nod. "Prime Minister."

In a quiet, resigned voice, I ordered the holo to turn off.

"Okay," I said. "Fill me in."

Winston filled me in. The problem started when religion was brought to their planet a little over a year ago. Instead of trying to better themselves, these people were trying to benefit materially from the work of our missionaries.

They thought our ship was there to negotiate a settlement—*hah*! I'd show them a settlement.

And what an ugly lot! They've got three eyes and no nose and a mouth too high on their egg-shaped heads. Not to mention sickly-green skin. One of them glared at me from the four-meter-high screen on the bridge.

"About time," he said.

"About time?" I said. "Are you so anxious to have your planet destroyed?"

The frown dropped from his face, then reappeared after the moment of shock passed. "What did you say?"

"Well, let's get on with it," I said, turning to my weapons officer. "Destroy this excuse for a planet."

My weapons officer nodded and started keying in the command to launch torpedoes. I hoped Winston had briefed him and he knew that I was just bluffing. If not, I figured, it'd be his neck and Winston's, not mine. And this current predicament would pretty much have resolved itself.

"Wait!" the Prime Minister said. "Stop!"

I turned to face the screen.

"Yes?" I said, impatiently.

"You can't do this!" he said. "We're supposed to negotiate a deal!"

"Okay," I said. "Stop bothering the Board and your planet doesn't vaporize to dust just yet. Deal?"

They didn't have spaceships or satellites or any other way to defend themselves. My weapons officer's finger was poised over the launch button. He had a hungry look on his face.

With a resigned sigh, the Prime Minister nodded.

I motioned to my communications officer to take the Minister's ugly mug off the screen.

Later that day, the report came in from the Board. Evaluations at Meekton showed a drop in gee-oh-vee. It was hovering just above nine-point-oh, and dropping. Not bad for a day's work; at the very least, it gave the Board time to decide what their next move would be.

Even though I had missed a good chunk of this week's *Captain Courageous*, I was happy. The Meek might indeed inherit the Earth—but not on my watch they won't.

Three

Lost Time

T HERE'S something that confuses me," my second-in-command Winston said, when on the holo Captain Courageous turned to wink at the cameras and the scene faded to black.

I figured Winston had never had the talk (shame on his father), so I began to prepare myself mentally to share my vast experience-based knowledge with him.

"You want to know why he winked at us, or what they're planning to do, the good captain and his scantily-clad, green-skinned companion?"

"What?" Winston said. Prior indiscretions had made me request a replacement for him, but Winston had grown on me since then. I made a mental note to remember to cancel the transfer request. "No."

"Then what?" I said.

"The Grumbles-Against-Earth ratings. Some people call them *gee-ah-vee* and others call them *gee-oh-vee*. Which one is it? *Ah* or *oh*? And what's the *vee* stand for? Shouldn't it be *gee-ah-eee* or *tee* or something?"

I stared at him. I made a mental note to remember to not remember to cancel the request to have Winston transferred out. Anyone who had the time to think about such things was not someone I wanted as first officer.

"That's a good point, Winston," I said, standing up, which was his cue to leave.

After he'd gone, I sunk back into my chair and wondered when I'd get some rest. Two episodes ago—*Captain Courageous* played on a weekly schedule—my crew and I had taken some lost time. It was unauthorized leave, of course—how else could *I* get vacation time?—so when the call from the Board came, it was me and me alone who went back to work, taking care of some rowdy colonists in an efficient but humane way. It was such a close call that I'd sworn off ever taking any more lost time.

My wallowing in self-pity was interrupted by a beep from the desk, followed by a drawn-out gurgling sound, like a cat dying slowly but painfully. I pushed off the obstructions—papers and books and a Captain Courageous figurine—freeing the screen, which emerged from the desk.

"Admiral Ed!" I said. His face had already materialized; he'd probably been staring at oak for the last minute.

"Long time no see, Wick," Ed said.

The good admiral calls me Wick because that was my nickname in the Academy. I earned the name because I was hot as a lit wick (and not because I was stringy as a wick, as some—the admiral, for example—would tell it). He calls me Wick because it's a reminder of the good old days, and of the closeness we share now because of the closeness we shared then. And also because he's an idiot who can't let an old joke die.

"So what's the good news, *Admiral*?" I said, stressing his new title. His promotion had come as a blow to me; *I* had been voted Most Likely to Succeed (and legitimately so, without tampering with the tabulation program in any way whatsoever, as some—the admiral, for example—would tell it).

"I'm leaving for Prima next week," the admiral said. "And I'd like you to come with me. We can tell old stories about the Academy days. You can make up stuff about the girls you dated back then, and I'll pretend to believe you."

I looked at him suspiciously. How had he known I'd been thinking about vacationing? Maybe the doctor ratted me out, I thought; told the Board I have high blood pressure; he's stressed out, needs a break. That rotten liar! That scoundrel! I'd skipped all my physicals; how could he know if I was stressed out or not?

"You got clearance for me?" I said. I'd used up all my leave time and more several years ago, chasing a treasure that wasn't there to be found. If I worked the next ten years straight, I still wouldn't work off half my debt.

"No," the admiral said, and I felt my heart sink. "But I can get it. I'm an admiral now, remember?" He winked at me.

But the next day, he didn't look so smug.

"No clearance, huh?" Somehow, it didn't feel so bad. It was good for Ed to be chopped down to size, even if it meant I wouldn't be going to Prima.

"Sorry, Wick. But it won't go through the system, you know? Not until your leave is out of the red."

"I guess it's true what they say, eh?"

"What's that?" the admiral said, though I felt he already knew.

Reaching to cut the connection, I said glumly, "No rest for the Wick, Ed."

Four

Lost Word

J<small>ACK</small>," I said, forcing a smile as my brother didn't fail to materialize on the middle pad in the teleportation room. Teleportation was safe, but, once every billion times, something would go wrong and the particles would be scattered throughout the universe. The person's body, life, personality, thought, condescension . . . all would be lost forever.

"*Bonjour*, Wick." Jack's eyes were bloodshot and he stumbled as he stepped down from the pad, but it was due to the effects of being teleported, I knew. Jack was too perfect to ever drink past his limit.

Ignoring his use of my nickname (because I'm a bigger man), I said, "Welcome to my humble warship, Jack. Classification: galaxy; maximum speed: oh-four-two; maximum firepower level: planet-destruction."

"*Impressionnant*," he said, but didn't look like he really thought so.

I grimaced. My crew and I had spent the last week

on hands and knees and ladders, scrubbing floors, bulk-
heads, and ceilings in anticipation of his arrival. We'd
been so busy cleaning, we'd even ignored three distress
signals and spent hours wiping all traces of the calls from
our logs. But it was wasted effort, it seemed. If Jack noticed how everything around us sparkled in its cleanliness,
he didn't seem to care. Maybe if we'd spent our time writing out the complete works of Guy de Maupassant on the
walls of my ship instead, I thought, maybe then he'd notice.

Taking his briefcase, I said, "So how's the family, Jack?"

"*Très bien*," he said. Then, as if for my benefit: "Very
well." Then, for his distinct benefit: "Marie says 'Allo.'"

The way God had planned the universe, Marie was
supposed to marry me. The first time I laid eyes on her—
she had come to pick up Jack for their date—I knew she
was the one for me.

"*I'm* Jack," I told her at the time. "I'll be ready to go
in just a few minutes."

She smiled and told me I was cute. Then, just as I had
warmed her up and was about to move in for the kill, here
comes Jack in his tweed jumpsuit and carrying his book
of French poetry. And there I went, kicked aside like a
doorstop that's no longer needed; and there they went, to
their date, to their marriage, to their happy life together.

"'Allo' right back," I said. "Sorry I couldn't make it to
the wedding."

Jack shrugged. "That was ten years ago."

"Has it been that long?"

He nodded.

Now that his eyes were no longer as bloodshot, I saw
that Jack had had them surgically altered: tiny words were

printed on each eyeball. The letters were translucent blue in color, hard to see the first time around but impossible to ignore once you'd noticed them. Looking into Jack's eyes, one literally saw poetry.

"Nice eyes," I said, my voice full of sarcasm and disdain.

"*Merci*, Jim," he said, with a little smile. "Marie likes them a lot." After a brief pause, he said, "It's a piece I wrote myself, *intitulé* 'The Lost Word of the Lifelong Lover.'"

I read the poem while Jack tried to stand still and not blink.

"So what is it?" I said, when I was done reading.

"What?"

"The lost word. What is it?"

"*Ah, le mot perdu.* It's whatever you think it is, as the reader. That's the beauty of it. In reading the poem, and coming up with an answer to what the lost *mot* might be, you learn as much about yourself as you do about the author. You in fact become co-author of the poem."

"Fascinating," I said.

We stepped into the chute and rose to the top floor. Once in my ready room, I offered Jack the seat in front of my desk.

Jack looked at it questioningly; the chair was very low to the ground. Gently I reminded him that there were species in this universe who weren't blessed, like him, with legs.

He took the seat quietly and opened his briefcase on his lap. I walked around the table and sat at my regular-sized captain's chair.

Jack tried to place a binder on the desk between us. His head barely reached above the edge of the table. He looked so ridiculous in that tiny chair that I was glad I was having the whole thing videotaped. My first officer Winston had made the chair the perfect size—not too low, not too high. Winston was back in my good books. It was all I could do to stop myself from bursting out in laughter. Jack was so ridiculous and so gullible—as if I'd let any legless species enter my ready room!

I wasn't laughing when Jack finally managed to push the binder across the table.

"What's this, a book?" I said.

"Just read it, *s'il vous plaît*," he said.

After reading the first paragraph, I said, "It's all like this? All seventy pages?" It was the most boring, driest writing I'd read since Jack used to show me his poetry in high school.

"*Oui.*"

"Then no," I said. "I refuse." Pushing the papers away from me, I continued: "I didn't want to sell the house anyway, especially not to *these* people, for whom a good old electronic signature isn't good enough. Besides, that home is filled not only with our own personal childhood memories, but with centuries of family history. It's a monument and it should stay within our family, with *us*, in the custodianship into which it was entrusted, to be treasured by our descendants for ages to come."

"Your take is on the last page," Jack said.

My take *was* the last page.

After I'd signed the papers, I said, half-heartedly, "You sure you can't stay longer, Jack?"

"*Non*," Jack said, putting the binder in his briefcase and—tragically—getting up from the hilariously tiny chair. "Marie awaits."

Jack couldn't say three words without mentioning her name, it seemed. I walked him back to the teleporter room and waited long enough to hear the confirmation from his ship. That was twice he'd teleported now, but no jackpot.

Later that day, Winston and I watched the recording I'd made and howled over how ridiculous Jack looked. The video only got funnier the more beers we had. But then Winston said something stupid and jumped right back into my bad books, undoing all the good he'd done in building that tiny chair.

We'd been laughing at Jack and I mentioned the translucent letters in his eyes and his stupid poem. But Winston stopped laughing and told me, in his tongue-loosened, artificially-brave drunken state, that my poems weren't much better.

"So?" I said, trying to focus my eyes on him, in case I decided I wanted to punch him.

"So," Winston said, slurring his words a little. "You should get yourself fixed up—you know?—before you look cri-*hic!*-tically at the *mot* in your brother's eye."

Five

Lost Ship

THE week got off to a bad start when I checked the listings beamed from Yoo and saw that this week's episode of *Captain Courageous and the Women Who Love Him* would be a repeat. A week without a new *Captain Courageous* to look forward to was a week best spent in bed.

But with an interstellar war raging in the depths of space, I had to captain my warship and not sulk. Or so my first officer, Winston, kept insisting. By Wednesday, I couldn't ignore his nagging anymore and finally tossed off the covers.

"Very well, Winston," I said. "Despite the crushing disappointment I've suffered, somehow I've found the strength to pull myself together again. Your captain is returned to you."

I slapped him on the shoulder and went to shower and shave while Winston returned to the bridge. Although I had already requested a transfer for Winston, I now decided to recall those orders. Winston had done a splendid job covering for me over the last few days. The Captain's Logs he'd filed by cutting and splicing audio from my previous logs were so convincing I half-believed them myself! (Then again, that he'd lie to protect his commanding officer meant that Winston had a devious streak; I must remember to take note of that character trait in his next performance report).

When I strode onto the bridge, Winston said loudly, "Battled off that nasty virus, have you, Captain?"

I had no idea what he was talking about. "I haven't been sick, Winston," I started to say. Then I looked around at the other officers. "By which I mean, I have indeed been sick, and am still very, very ill, but it'll take more than some bug to keep me off my own bridge for more than a few days."

Led by Winston, the officers cheered. I can be pretty quick-thinking under pressure.

"Status report," I said to Winston when I sat down in the captain's chair.

"A small ship, perhaps from the Other Side, has trespassed into our space. We're on an intercept course, ETA two hours."

The ship was very tiny indeed—so small it didn't even have a weapons system. Personally, I'd be embarrassed to captain a ship like that. Although size isn't everything, my ship was thirty times the size of theirs, which is something.

"Hail them," I said. Then: "You have one second to identify yourselves or we will destroy you."

Although I am by nature a pacifist, I had a feeling that this ship was from the Other Side, and those people only respond to threats of violence. True to form, before the full second had passed, the ship returned our hail.

"Pleese don't deestroy us," they said in that peculiar Other Side accent. "Wee are a reesearch sheep gone eestray, a modeest veessel. Wee got lost in thee Peebular system, wheere thee radiation preeved too much for our meegre deefences. Without navigation seestems, wee treed to feend our way home, but obviously miscaluleeted."

Winston leaned across and whispered in my ear. "We should escort them back to Other Side space. This is a great opportunity to extend an olive branch, a goodwill gesture that may be the beginning of the end of this bloody war."

Winston had a way of saying things that made me angry. Who said anyone wanted an end to this bloody war? Certainly no one serving on my ship, a *warship*. What use was there for a warship or its captain in peacetime? I saw past Winston's words to the insubordination underneath.

But this time, there was more to my displeasure than Winston's regular rebellion. Here was a golden opportunity floating right beneath his nose, but Winston couldn't see it for what it was. It doesn't bode well for my succession plan when the Board finally wakes up and realizes what a great admiral I'd make.

I stood up with so much force that I almost knocked Winston to the ground.

"Ship thirty times smaller than mine!" I said. "Prepare to be boarded. Anyone who resists will be shot with lethal weapons, as those are the only kind we carry. Anyone who seems to resist will also be shot, as we can't take chances and my security personnel are a trigger-happy bunch. My suggestion is that you all lie face down—now is a good time—and be completely still while my crew boards your ship."

To his credit, Winston gave the order to assemble and make ready a boarding party before turning to me and saying, "Captain, I don't understand."

"And that's why I'm captain and you're not, Winston." In fact, Winston had me down as a reference, so I knew how many times he'd been up for the position. And if it was something I'd said that caused him to be passed over all those times—well, I'm not about to apologize for telling the truth.

"Captain?" Winston said.

"Hm? Oh, yes. Like I was saying, this is a great find. We'll take it back to Earth and reap the rewards." If this isn't worth an admiralty, I thought, I don't know what is.

"I still don't understand, Captain."

"Don't you read the Bible, Winston?"

Winston nodded, but I knew he was lying.

"If you read the Bible, Winston, you'd know that there's nothing quite like finding a lost sheep."

Six

Lost Opportunity

IN my long and distinguished career, I have seen many admirals snarl, scowl, swear, and shake their heads in disappointment. But I'd never seen one this angry before.

"This is a disaster, Kollins," Admiral Potrowski said, spitting in his anger and pounding his clenched fist against the desk in front of him. "This is an unmitigated disaster."

"I agree with you, sir," I said, wiping away spittle that had landed on my forehead. "When we found the ship, I was bedridden—ill with a nasty virus. My first officer was in charge; it was his decision to bring the lost ship back to Earth. Had he chosen to consult with me, even in my state, I would have advised him to escort the ship back to Other Side space, as a show of goodwill."

The admiral shook his head slowly, seeming to calm a little with each swing of his neck. "If only, Captain." With a tired and wistful sigh, he added, "We really lost an opportunity here. Returning that ship might have helped put an end to this bloody war."

"And isn't that what we all want, Admiral?"

My words seemed to snap the admiral out of his pensive mood. Standing up, he said, "You're captain of the *DeVille*, Kollins. You must be held accountable for its actions."

"Of course, sir," I said, cursing the admiral silently but colorfully in my head.

"You and your crew will remain in this system until the Board can think of an appropriate punishment. As you can imagine, we've got our hands full doing damage control for this disaster you've brought on our heads."

"Yes, sir." I turned to leave.

"Captain."

I turned around slowly.

"Don't worry about your first officer," the admiral said. "This blunder of his won't soon be forgotten."

"He's young and inexperienced," I said, deferentially. "I hope the Board takes that into consideration when deciding his fate, sir."

"You're a good captain, Kollins," the admiral said, softening a little. "But don't allow your affection for this Winston to take you down with him."

With a nod, I turned once more and walked out of the admiral's office.

My senior staff was waiting for me at the Tiberia, a bar in Luna City that catered mostly to officers of the Board.

Their expectant smiles faded as I walked through the doorway, my shoulders drooping and a sour look on my face.

"Bad news?" Winston said.

"I don't know," I said, suddenly slapping him on the back and smiling as wide as my lips would allow. "Would you consider it bad news that the Board is so thrilled with our capture, they're rewarding us with some vacation time?"

With a cheer, the senior officers raised their glasses in my name and I graciously suffered their pats on my back.

"Listen," I said, turning very serious. "They'll need to make a show of disapproval. The Other Side has spies everywhere, and if they thought the Board was happy with this capture—which they are, they are!—that might cause the Other Side to escalate this war before the Board is ready for them. Just be aware that anything you hear is for show only; deep down, the Board is thrilled with us."

Again they raised their drinks and again they cheered my name.

When the other officers were gone, Winston turned to me with a very serious look on his face and said, "I was wrong, Captain."

Despite his time with me, Winston had never learned the crucial lesson that one never admitted it when one was wrong. "It takes a big man to say that," I said. "Good for you and forget about it. I know I have."

"Thank you, Captain."

"We all make mistakes, Winston. The important thing is to learn from them."

"Yes, Captain," he said. "I guess I was just anxious for peace—"

"Isn't that what we're all anxious for?" I interrupted.

"It is, Captain. But you were able to maintain your objectivity, and I allowed my feelings to cloud my thinking." Winston was becoming very depressed, which usually didn't happen until he'd had a lot more to drink. "May I speak freely, Captain?"

I nodded graciously.

"Most captains don't make decisions all by themselves," Winston said. "They consult, they listen to their first officers and advisers. They think things through. But you . . . you seem to know exactly what to do without talking to anyone else, and even when"—here he became very sheepish—"you're given bad advice."

"Some may question my management style," I said, mentally noting that Winston himself had obviously questioned it, yet another sign of his ever-present insubordination. "But I've learned an important lesson, a lesson you might learn too if only you read the Good Book."

"Oh?"

"It's very simple," I said. "I keep my own counsel; that way, I will always have the wisdom of a solo man."

Seven

Lost Reward

WHEN the last of my crew had left the ship, off to visit family and friends and mistresses, I made ready to pilot the *DeVille* myself. The Board could take all the time in the world to decide my punishment, I figured, but I wasn't fool enough to be around when they made up their minds. In a large universe such as ours, there are more than enough places to escape to, places where one can change one's name and appearance, places where one can live out a whole new life, a life that didn't include whatever punishment the Board had cooked up for one in their depraved minds.

It didn't even occur to me to wonder if my punishment would be worse if the Board caught me trying to escape... until the console on my chair's armrest beeped. I hadn't made it past Jupiter and already they'd caught me.

For an instant, I considered ignoring the beep. But whatever the Board already had in mind, I knew, it couldn't be worse than having hundreds of the Board's ships de-

33

scend on me and turn my ship into a dust cloud of insubordination.

"Yes?" I said, touching the contact on my armrest and
trying to make my voice sound casual.

Admiral Potrowski's face appeared on the main screen,
looking nowhere near as angry as I expected.

"Captain," he said, his voice mild and curious. "Didn't
I give you strict orders to remain on Earth?"

"Yes, sir. But we were getting anomalous readings
from the ship's engines; I wanted to run them around for
a while, to discover the source of the problem."

The admiral looked unconvinced for a moment, but
then he shrugged it off. "Whatever, Kollins. Not even
your regular defiance can make me angry with you right
now. All thanks to your first officer."

"Winston?"

"Do you have any other first officers you haven't told
us about, Captain?" I'd never before heard the admiral
make a joke. "Yes, of course, Winston. Put him on, will
you?"

"I can't," I said, cringing as the admiral's face clouded
over. "Due to the dangerous nature of these tests I'm running on the ship's engines, I ordered my crew off the ship."

"Well how do we reach him?" the admiral said, full of
enough excitement and happiness to make anyone—even
someone as equanimous as myself—want to burst with
anger. "There's a celebration in his honor and a captain-
ship waiting for him, his choice of any vessel in the fleet!"

"What? Why? What's happened?"

"What's happened is that the ship Winston captured
and brought back to the Board—the ship that you would

have returned to Other Side space—was not a research vessel at all."

"No?" I said, gulping.

"No. Do you know who we found aboard the ship?"

"Who?" I closed my eyes and prayed that the admiral would say any name except "Dr. Evan."

"Dr. Evan, that's who! He was disguised, of course: different skin color, different height, different build. But DNA isn't so easily disguised. And I think I can tell you, Captain, without offending my modesty, that it was my idea and my order to run everyone through the tests."

"Evan!" I said, cursing. One of our top-ranking military scientists, Evan had gone missing a few weeks before. It was hoped that he'd been murdered and dumped into deep space; it was feared that he had defected to the Other Side. Too recently, another research scientist named Urth had tried to defect to the Other Side. I myself had entertained hopes of capturing Dr. Urth and bringing him back, but that honor went to my long-time friend—and once fellow captain—Ed, who for his efforts got an immediate promotion to a nice, cushy admiralty, where he could sit on his butt and watch episodes of *Captain Courageous* all day.

"We've already contacted the Other Side and they're disavowing all knowledge of the ship and its crew, sure confirmation that this mission to help Dr. Evan defect goes all the way to the top levels of the Other Side government."

"Evan!" I said. His capture was a gold-find, an instant promotion—but now my witless first officer was getting the credit and the reward, even though both rightfully belonged to me.

"Get in touch with your first officer, Captain," the admiral said. "You can tell him the good news yourself."

"Admiral," I said, forcing my voice to sound calm and steady. "There's something I have to tell you about my first officer Winston."

"Yes?"

"He's dead, sir."

"Dead?"

"Yes."

"How?"

"By his own hand. Winston had many faults, one of which was a cowardly disposition. Unable to live like a man, to face the consequences of his actions as we all must, he chose instead to end his own life."

"No!"

"Yes."

"What a tragedy."

"Indeed, Admiral. Very tragic. But we need to keep this quiet, to protect his memory and his family. As luck would have it, Winston has a twin brother I can hire for the post of first officer; no one need know about Winston's— the dead Winston's—act of shameful cowardice."

"Winston has a twin brother?"

"Yes."

"A twin brother you're going to hire to be your new first officer?"

"Yes." He stared at me for a very long time; I could almost hear his thoughts. Maybe Winston hadn't committed suicide—but maybe he had. Maybe Winston's suicide wouldn't be blamed on the admiral and his ominous threats—but maybe it would. In cases like this, it was best not to ask too many questions and just leave things nice and covered up.

He shrugged. "As you think best, Captain."

"Thank you, sir."

When the admiral's face disappeared from the screen, I sunk into my captain's chair with a sigh. It was close, but I had managed to save Winston's immortal soul. Had I allowed Winston to attend a celebration in his honor and receive a captaincy and his choice of ship in the fleet—all on false pretenses—I would have made out of him a liar and a thief of the credit that rightly belonged to me.

Yet I couldn't deny that I was disappointed. Once, I had missed my chance to be rewarded in Urth; now, I wouldn't be rewarded in Evan either.

Eight

Lost Empire

GATHERING my crew back to my ship was much harder than it should have been. If I was away on vacation and my boss was looking for me, I wouldn't answer my phone either, but really, I expected more from them.

Eventually I tracked them all down and we were ready to get underway.

"Neat mission, eh, Winston?" I said to my first officer, the next day. We were escorting the ship we'd captured back to Other Side space. Of course, we weren't sending it back with its original crew.

"I don't know, Captain."

"What do you mean? It's brilliant. They were helping Dr. Evan defect to their side; well, if they want him so badly, we'll give him to them. Or at least, someone who looks just like him."

"That's just it, Captain," Winston-the-worrywart said. "What if they figure it out? This could escalate the war to disastrous proportions. We should have sent the ship and crew back, minus Dr. Evan. The ceasefire we have is tenuous at best, but it has averted immeasurable bloodshed in the last few months. Don't you think this could jeopardize all of that? I just can't escape the feeling that this is a dangerous game we're playing. We might not have that much to gain and we have so much to lose."

I was accustomed to Winston's constant second-guessing, but this was getting to be too much. How could I work with a first officer whose main joy in life was spoiling any enthusiasm I cared to show? It all made me so mad I wanted to scream at him.

"You raise a very good point, Winston," I said. "However, we have our orders and I intend to carry them out."

"Of course, Captain. But it's not too—"

Whatever insolent phrase Winston was about to say never made it out of his mouth.

"Captain," Nikki, my very beautiful and long-legged, although tragically not green-skinned, tactical officer said.

"Yes?" I said, turning my gaze—very happily—away from Winston and onto Nikki.

"We're being followed, sir. The ship just appeared on my screen, but it's gaining on us at an incredible rate."

Despite his tendency toward worrywarting, Winston was good under pressure.

"Silent alert," he said immediately. If I were stranded on a desert island and could only pick one person to be with me, Winston would be my last choice. But if I were stranded on a desert island *and* was being attacked by savages *and* had run out of food *and* could only pick one person *and* it couldn't be a woman, Winston would be close to the top of the list.

"What do you think, Winston?" I said, speaking low enough that only he could hear me.

"We're still too far away from Other Side space for this to be one of their ships," he said, whispering back. Despite his words, Winston looked and sounded worried.

"We're a warship, Winston," I said, trying to reassure him. "Or have you forgotten?" I turned to my tactical officer and said, "Nikki, what can you tell me about that ship?"

Nikki's slender fingers flew over her console. "It's a small ship, about the size of one of our scouts. I'm not reading any weapons systems, but the energy signature is unlike anything I've ever seen before. And it's almost on top of us."

"Full alert," I said.

"Captain," Winston said. "I suggest we stay on silent alert."

"Oh?"

"We don't know who or what is inside that ship. Maybe they've got hostile intentions, but maybe they don't. Going to full alert might send the wrong message."

My security officer was waiting.

"Stay at silent alert." Whispering, I said to Winston, "This flight plan you wrote—did you look into the systems we'd be going through?"

Winston nodded. "All of these systems are supposed to be uninhabited. We're in the"—he checked the console on his chair—"Stratocat system." He paused again, pressing several contacts on the console. "There hasn't been a ship to fly through here in a hundred years. And that ship did so without incident."

"We're being hailed, Captain," my communications officer said.

"On screen."

Nikki made an "aww" sound as the view on the mainscreen switched from a star field to a little man in a little chair. He looked like a human baby, complete with a bald head with tiny wisps of hair and several rolls under his dimpled chin.

The baby spoke gobbledygook until we could get the translator tuned correctly. Finally he said, "Can you hear me now?"

"My name is Captain James Kollins of the warship *DeVille*," I said. "Identify yourself."

"My name is Lon," he said, sending shivers down my spine. "I come from a system not far from here; I am an emissary on a mission to find other civilizations."

Despite the thoughts racing through my mind, I managed to keep my cool. "Yes, of course you are, Lon. And what is it you're supposed to do with these civilizations once you find them?"

The little baby looked surprised at the question, as if he didn't know what I was getting at. "Why, to form a relationship of course. We wish to exchange ideas, trade goods, share experiences, and learn from one another."

"That sounds great," I said, ignoring for the moment the indignity of a little baby lying to my face. "That's exactly what we want too. Are you authorized to provide me with the coordinates of your home-world?"

"Of course I am." The baby pushed some buttons on his console; a moment later, my communications officer nodded. We had them.

"That's fantastic, Lon. We have to go now, because we're on an important mission. But I'm going to send one of our emissaries to your home-world, and we can negotiate a treaty and do all that other good stuff you talked about. Sound okay?"

"Yes!" the little baby said, almost jumping in his seat out of excitement. "I think this is the beginning of a great friendship."

"Oh, me too," I said, cutting the connection.

Winston turned to me. "This is incredible, Captain. We've discovered a new species and laid the foundation for a cultural exchange that will benefit both of our civilizations."

"This is a greater opportunity than you think, Winston. Send the board a top-priority message."

"Captain?"

"Tell them to assemble every fighting ship in the fleet."

"I don't understand."

"Tell them to descend on the coordinates we give them and obliterate Lon's homeworld before that evil civilization of his has the slightest chance to destroy us first."

"What?" Winston said, his voice full of despair and confusion.

"Tell them," I said, with a heavy sigh, "that we've engaged the lost empire of Baby Lon."

Nine

Lost Prayer

WINSTON had graduated from passive insubordination to outright defiance. Despite my orders to warn the Board of the existence of an ancient and evil civilization, Winston refused to send the message.

We spent two hours in heated argument. But then it was almost time for *Captain Courageous and the Women Who Love Him* and I said, "Winston, you've convinced me."

"I have?"

"Yes indeed." I spoke quickly; I didn't have much time before the intro song to *Captain Courageous* came on. "You send whatever message you think is appropriate."

Winston looked so relieved that I wondered if he too were eager to get to his quarters and to this week's *Captain Courageous*. But he spoiled whatever respect I had for him by saying, "Thank you, Captain. I think we've just saved the lives of billions of people."

"That's great," I said. "Now off you go." I shooed him out of my office just in time for the intro song. As I always do, in my carefree and fun-loving way, I sang along:

> *Women love him, so do men,*
> *But men in a non-sexual way;*
> *His ship is huge, his brain is large;*
> *His step is sure, he's never wrong;*
> *His smile is wide, his hair is nice;*
> *He's braver than brave,*
> *   and stronger than strong,*
> *He's Captain—He's Captain—*
> *   He's Captain Cou-ra-geous!*

But like so many things in my life lately, *Captain Courageous* proved to be a disappointment—another week, another repeat. By this time, disappointment was such a constant companion that it only took a few hours for me to recover from the depression I suffered due to the non-new nature of this week's episode. It is indeed true that what doesn't kill us only makes us stronger.

I went back to my bridge. "Status?"

"The ship has just entered Other Side space," Winston said. "They'll be out of range within the hour; after that, if anything happens, they'll be on their own."

I shook my head. "What kind of talk is that, Winston? Don't you know that even when we're alone, we're not really alone."

"You're right. Sorry, Captain."

When the hour was up, Winston said, "We have orders to rendezvous with the *Spirit*."

"Warship?" I said.

"No, they're priests."

"What are our orders?"

"To escort them to the Stavinsky system and protect them while they carry out their work. A conference for the local priests, I think."

I smiled. Stavinsky was violently anti-religious. This could be fun; it had been far too long since I'd fired my ship's weapons.

But we spent four days without incident; just watching over the *Spirit* and waiting for some kind of violent outburst we could squelch. No such luck.

"Thank you, Captain," the priest Pedro said at the end of the four days.

"We'll escort you back to Fajer," I said, trying to make the offer sound innocent.

"You've done more than enough, Captain. I think we'll be safe finding our own way home."

"I insist."

On the screen, Pedro's giant head nodded. "As you wish, Captain."

"That was awfully nice of you," Winston said, when the screen dimmed.

"Nice has nothing to do with it," I said, whispering. "I've got a long list of things I need to ask God for."

Winston gave me a cross look. "Captain, first of all, prayer should be about more than asking God for things. Second, you can pray anywhere and everywhere. You don't have to be in a particular system to speak with God."

"Oh no," I said. "I've tried that pray-anywhere thing and it doesn't work. The other day, I begged God for a new *Captain Courageous* and this week—another repeat. But I've spent the last several hours thinking this through: I've got a plan that's bound to succeed."

Back in my office, I went over my list again, making sure I hadn't left anything off. That I'd get some new *Captain Courageous* episodes? Check. That I'd get my long-overdue promotion? Check. That Marie would leave Jack? Check and double-check.

Winston's voice came through the intercom: "We're there, Captain."

"On screen," I said, running onto the bridge. "I want to see their homeworld, the sun, and their ship—all at once, all on the same screen."

When my tactical officer Nikki complied, I kneeled in front of the screen and began to pray. I'd spent so much time looking over my list that I didn't even need to refer to it. I had thirty-three requests, and I had memorized them all. When I was finished, I stood and told Winston to get us back on course for our next mission.

"I hope you took advantage of that, Winston."

"Captain?"

"Did you pray just now?"

"No, Captain."

"Too bad," I said. "You lost a marvelous opportunity."

"I don't understand."

"Winston, when do you ever understand anything without me having to explain it to you?"

"But this time I'm really confused," Winston said. "I mean, you just knelt down and prayed to a planet and a ship. How is that such a special opportunity?"

"It's 'kneeled' not 'knelt'," I corrected softly. "And I didn't kneel down and pray to a planet and a ship; I kneeled down and prayed to the Fajer, the sun, and the holy *Spirit*."

Ten

Lost Show

Iɴ the face of obstacles and challenges, a true leader shows initiative and courage.

As I dialed up some tea and settled into my comfiest chair to watch the latest *Captain Courageous*, and saw that once again it was a repeat, I stared dumbfounded at the viewscreen on my wall. "No," I said, though of course no one was around to hear me, except Winston. "Not again. This can't keep happening to me. I prayed! I didn't even bother to check the listings! I prayed!"

Winston got up.

"You're leaving?"

"It's a repeat," Winston said, heading for my quarter's doors. "I've seen this one. I'll be on the bridge if you need me."

I wanted to tell him to watch it again—Winston still hadn't come to appreciate *Captain Courageous* as much as I needed a first officer serving under me to—but I knew he was right. Repeats were well and good when one had a few hours to kill; it was a yearly ritual for me to book my annual health checkup as late in the year as possible, then spend the rest of the day hiding in an air duct with a portable viewer, watching episodes until the next day, when a new year had begun and it was too late to file a checkup report for the old year. But repeats were not well and good when one was expecting a new episode.

Did I allow the depression to overwhelm me? Did I allow the crushing disappointment to squeeze out all the energy and life from me?

No. I took the UpUGo to the bridge (incidentally, my grandfather knew the inventor of the UpUGo and even tried to get her to change its name on the basis that it went up, down, and all around, but apparently UpDownAndAllAroundUGo was too cumbersome for her tastes; he was so insistent that his name for it was better, though, that they broke things off and two generations later I wouldn't inherit an embarrassing family fortune. On the other hand, no family fortune meant I had to work for a living; and my work put me in charge of considerable resources. And where some men can do no more than shake their heads in impotent frustration, I am not some men; I am the captain of a warship).

"Captain on the bridge!" I said, before anyone else could. A true leader doesn't wait around for others. "Pat, set a course for Yoo immediately. Full power."

Winston moved over to the first officer's chair. When I sat down in the captain's, he leaned over and whispered, "Sir, are you sure this is wise? We're supposed to be on patrol."

I ignored him, and eventually he sat back in his chair. No new *Captain Courageous* meant that none of my prayers had worked. Marie would stay with Jack, I'd stay a captain, Winston wouldn't commit treason and I wouldn't be the hero who, despite personal feelings, captured and turned him in due to my unassailable integrity.

But God helps those who help themselves, I told myself. It was possible this latest setback was a test.

"I won't fail, Winston," I said, but of course Winston just gave me a quizzical look. Sometimes his lack of understanding, and need to have everything spelled out in minutest detail, stupefies me.

Yoo is a studio planet, where most of the actors and actresses of most of the shows beamed throughout the galaxy live and work; it is an artificial planet with snow-covered plains in the north and tropical jungles in the south, with underground villages and old-town cities of tall skyscrapers and road vehicles. *Captain Courageous* had its own city in the southern hemisphere, where Winston and I landed our shuttle.

"Hello!" a chipper young man said, walking toward us. "Mr. Brillig will see you whenever you're ready."

I stepped off the ship's ramp and onto the tarmac. "Now," I said.

Mr. Brillig's office was much larger than my ready room and quarters combined, which set me on edge as soon as we were ushered in. I saved lives (on our side) and destroyed lives (on the Other Side); he directed a holodrama—but *his* office is bigger than mine? Such is the topsy-turvy world we live in.

"Gentlemen," he said, as we sat in the chairs opposite his desk. "I'm very pleased to meet you. Captain Kollins, your letters have been a source of hilarity for many of us who work on the show."

"Of hilarity?" I said, speaking through clenched jaw.

"Well—yes, we get the joke of course. Surely you weren't being—"

"I meant every word," I said. "Though of course I must say—as a matter of professional respect and honest criticism—that the show under your predecessor was in some ways smarter, funnier, and cleverer—and in all other ways better."

Mr. Brillig looked down at his desk and seemed to be holding back something, perhaps tears. After a moment, he pulled himself together and said, "Well, anyway, that isn't why you're here, is it? Tell me about the emergency situation."

I couldn't help but notice that Winston's head snapped to the right so he could stare at me with his judgmental eyes. Yes, I'd lied to get us immediate permission to land on the planet; yes, I said that there was an emergency, life-and-death situation and that I had to speak to the direc-tor of *Captain Courageous* personally. Yes, I'd "abused my power" and "caused a panic needlessly," but Winston could only judge me because he's never loved anything as much as I love *Captain Courageous*.

"You're not asking the questions here, Director." I fixed him with a suspicious glare. "Why haven't you been releasing new episodes of *Captain Courageous*?"

For all his smarminess and largess of office, Mr. Bril-lig was speechless.

"There's no emergency," Winston said. His knack for stating the obvious never failed to astonish me. "The Cap-tain just really likes your show."

Mr. Brillig looked from one of us to the other. "I—really, you came all the way over here just to ask about the show?"

"I have a ship," I said. "Just like Captain Courageous. And I don't pay for my own fuel. So, yes, we came all the way over here. Now answer the question."

A tenseness seized Mr. Brillig's features. He put his hands in front of him on the desk. "Ken Treme is sick."

"By 'sick' you mean 'good,' right?" I said hopefully. Treme had played Captain Courageous since the first season of the show, and I already knew he was good, very good—as did anyone who watched the show. But I hoped the director liked stating the obvious as much as my first officer.

"I mean ill. Very, very ill. We keep hoping to see a change for the better, but . . . it doesn't look good."

"That's very sad," Winston said.

Ignoring Mr. Obvious, I said, "We wish him a quick recovery. In the meantime, you must have new material that you can release."

"No, nothing," Brillig said. "We've aired it all. We even stitched together a bunch of outtakes of past shows and pretended it was a drug-induced dream Captain Courageous was having."

"Very powerful episode," I said, turning to face Winston. "Very important message."

"Anyway, we're done," Brillig said. "We're empty. We don't have a single new scene with Ken in it."

I sat up straight. "Not a single scene, you say?"

"No, not one."

I sat back and smiled. "Perfect, then. I know just what to do." I turned to Winston. "We're going to Eden."

"Eden? There's nothing left there."

"Not quite nothing," I said. "I have a friend there who may be willing to help us out." I stood, stuck out my hand. "Take heart," I said to Brillig. "Things will get better. Remember—blessed are those who believe, yet have not scene."

Eleven

Lost Everything

I DESCENDED to Eden alone, despite Winston's head-shaking, and retraced my steps from months before. But where I expected to find the large bush, I saw instead a middle-aged man sitting on a wooden chair painted white.

"Can I help you?" he said, turning to look at me.

My scanner showed no signs of Gamma Bamma radiation. "Have you seen a bush?" I said.

"A few," he said with a smile, waving his arms at the vegetation around us.

"This is a special bush," I said. "It emits a lot of radiation and speaks to you if you touch it."

"Why would you touch it?"

"Because a coward would fear touching it," I said, and couldn't help but puff out my chest a little, "and I'm brave."

The man nodded. "Have a seat, James."

For the first time I noticed a chair across from him. I took it.

"Are you Lord?" I said.

He nodded again.

"But you're human. And you're talking just fine."

"You've never really read the Bible, have you?"

I looked down. Tiny images of fish were etched into the wooden arm of the chair. "It's very long," I said, finally looking back at Lord. "I skimmed quite a lot of it. I read all the important bits." After a pause, I said, "Most of the important bits. Some of the letters at the back are tough going, they're hard to skim so I skipped them. Because I figured: who puts the important information at the back of a book? Right?"

"Did you come here to ask for eternal life again?"

I shook my head, knowing he wouldn't grant it to me anyway. "If you are anything like the Lord of the Bible," I said, "you know why I came here. So why do you ask?"

He smiled again. "You want me to heal Ken Treme so he can keep making new *Captain Courageous* episodes."

I leaned forward in my chair and placed my hand in my pocket where I ran my finger over the Captain Courageous figurine. "Will you?"

A darkness swept across his face. "I can't help you. I'm sorry to tell you that Ken Treme is dead."

"You can bring him back." I saw the dark look in his eyes. "But you won't, will you? Maybe you have no power at all."

He was silent.

"If you have power, prove it! Bring him back!"

He just stared at me. Above us, beams of sunlight struggled to pierce through the tall, leafy branches of the surrounding trees.

"Is it that you won't," I said, "or that you can't?" Ken Treme was dead. No more *Captain Courageous* ever again, at least not the same Captain Courageous I'd always known. "Why don't you say something?" No more *Captain Courageous*, ever. The reality of the statement was only slowly taking solid shape in my mind, but its weight was already threatening to crush me. "Please," I said, changing my tone. "I only want this. Please—I'm a good person, I deserve it."

Instantly, the man was out of his chair and over to mine, his right hand gripping my neck and his knee pressing onto my leg, holding me down. It happened so fast that I didn't have a chance to react.

"You're a good person?" he said, speaking through clenched teeth. "You destroyed an entire colony simply because you were ordered to do so, without a single pang of conscience or guilt."

"I—can—t—brea—the."

"You almost destroyed an entire civilization," he went on, oblivious to my suffering, "because of a stupid pun. You had a chance to end an interstellar war and save billions of lives, but your own greed and selfishness stopped you from acting on it. You hate your brother, for no greater crime than marrying a woman he loves and who loves him. And when I gave you the chance to reconcile, what did you do? You spent all of your time and energy trying to impress him and, as if your pettiness was trying to outdo itself, you forced him to sit in a ridiculously small chair. You refuse to see any good in Winston, who would be three times the captain you are, and used every trick of deceit and malice to hold back the promotion he deserves far more than you ever did."

His grip tightened and I started to lose consciousness. But what does it matter? I thought. I'd never see another *Captain Courageous*, which is the only thing that had given me any joy since I'd failed to steal Marie from Jack at their wedding.

"Tell me," Lord said, his voice seeming to come from far away, "does that sound like a good person to you?"

The breath had been choked out of me; I couldn't speak. Not when he puts it like that, it doesn't, I thought. That sounds more like "a horrible person. A self-centered, needy, angry, bitter, resentful person, ready to take offense at the slightest slight. And you'd have to add covetousness and lechery on top of that; he forgot to mention my many acts of wanton lust. Even as I pined for Marie, I devoured Nikki, a subordinate officer, with my eyes. Not to mention any number of other women, single and married and interested and usually not so interested."

Slowly I realized that I'd started speaking; that Lord was in his chair; that my throat and neck didn't hurt at all, as if he hadn't just choked me to within a centimeter of my life. Then the words Lord said finally registered. "What do you mean, you gave us the chance to reconcile?" After a moment's thought, I grasped the truth: Lord was the buyer who had demanded, inexplicably, a physical signature. Lord had orchestrated the meeting with my brother, and perhaps a lot of other things. Lord knew everything I'd done and thought since I met him in the bush and perhaps since the very beginning of my life.

"Don't spare me, then," I said. "I don't want to live anyway."

"Because of the loss of a holodrama?"

The sun's motion brought its rays below the tall branches,

and bright light seemed to flood the clearing where we spoke. I met Lord's eyes, remarkably kind eyes for someone who I felt sure was waiting to finish the job he'd started.

"How about because my life is so pathetic and empty a holodrama is all I have, and its loss brings me to despair?"

"As you wish," Lord said, and lifted his hand.

"Wait!" I said, ducking out of the line of sight of his extended finger, half expecting a laserbeam to come shooting out. "I didn't think you were actually going to do it! Well, before you incinerate me, can you at least satisfy my curiosity on a few things?"

"Like?"

"Why did you speak in broken sentences when we first met? Why would God—if that's who you are—not be able to understand simple English?"

"I spoke in the language you needed to hear. I hoped it would make you reevaluate your life, perhaps reawaken your conscience."

"But instead—"

"—instead you used your personal logs to make puns, sometimes arranging entire events just for the purpose of a silly payoff."

"I thought you liked puns," I said. "And figured I'd have it on record, as many times as possible, that I liked them too."

"Some of your puns were better than others," Lord, or the Lord, said.

"So that's it for me, then? I guess you said it yourself—Winston should be captain of the *DeVille*, Jack and Marie are happy and deserve one another, and no more *Captain Courageous* for me."

"It doesn't have to be it for you, James. I know that even as we speak, you're composing in your mind a log of today's events. For starters, don't even think about ending it with a pun. Second, I wasn't going to let you die just yet. You have a lot of wrongs to undo."

I thought I understood. I nodded, hesitantly at first and then with more energy. "Thank you," I said. "*Merci*," I continued, switching to French. Yes, I did understand now what I had to do. "*Merci*," I said again. "*Merci, merci, merci!*"

"Careful," the Lord said, but it was too late.

"You see?" I'd already started, and couldn't stop myself. "The conversion of my life has already begun! Just like you, Lord, I'm full of *merci*."

Twelve

... and Found

M^{Y} name is Thurstle Winston (*seriously, your first name is Thurstle, Winston? Why didn't I ever read your personnel file? Actually you're lucky I never did!*), and I am first officer of the galactic warship *DeVille* (*not so, old friend, you're captain now.*) Captain James Kollins has been missing for a full week.

When the captain (*you're the captain now*) insisted on descending to Eden alone, it went against my every instinct, not to mention a few regulations, to allow him to do so. But the captain (*you're the captain*) is a difficult person to disagree with normally, and he was not his normal self: I'd never before seen the kind of energy and determination he exhibited. I let him go alone, taking the quiet precaution of tracking his shuttle and then him himself (*"him himself," Winston? What kind of writing is that?*) as he trekked through a forested area on the east side of the planet. He came to a sudden stop in one place, no more or less interesting than any other, and stayed there for the better part of an hour. Just as my fears that something had happened to him began to overwhelm me, but before I could deploy a search and rescue party, the captain (*don't make me say it again*) began to move once more, with great speed, back toward the shuttlecraft. But once he was in the shuttle, both signals disappeared.

We've searched everywhere on the planet and in the system, and scanned as far as a shuttlecraft can travel in seven days. James Kollins is missing, and I am at fault. We keep searching, but I grow more despondent with every passing day, and feel that I can delay no longer. Tomorrow I will alert the Board of the situation, and will, of course, take full responsibility.

(*Stop sounding so gloomy, Winston! Everything is taken care of. And you're going to make a better captain than I ever did. All the paperwork has been submitted to the Board, backdated so it looks like I sent it in several months ago. Some clerk will discover the file, think the oversight and delay is his fault, and fast-track the approval. Your status will be official in a few days, I'm sure.*)

I SEE that somehow the captain (*you're the captain*) has changed my log (*yes, I have mad hacking skills. In high school, I modified the tabulation program so that any vote as Most Likely to Succeed cast for a close friend of mine was counted as a vote for me. Don't judge me too harshly, Winston; I was young and ambitious and had a conscience the size of a pea. Were I interested in defending my actions (I'm not), I might mention that someone who has the ability to break into the principal's computer and hack the tabulator without attracting attention, then walk away with enough blackmail material to ensure*

against the principal if his suspicion was aroused, de-
serves the title more than some goody-two-shoes, school-
liking, detention-not-getting, stupid-nickname-not-able-to-
let-go-of future admiral, don't you agree?) I appreciate
what you've done for me, sir, but I have so many questions. As a start, what happened to you on Eden?

(Well, Winston, when I was down on the planet's sur-
face, I realized something—or, to be honest, I realized a
few things. One is that I'd never given my brother and his
wife a wedding present. This upset me very much, and I
decided to rectify the situation without further delay. I
borrowed the shuttle and made my way back to Earth.
Hiding my signal from the DeVille*'s sensors was easy—I*
rigged them long ago so that I could mask my shuttlecraft
with the push of a button, if I ever needed to make an
escape. A captain can never take too many precautions
to prepare against mutinies, or so I thought at the time.
Finding ships that were headed in the right direction, and
piggybacking a ride without being discovered, was quite
a different story. But once I've set my mind to something,
Winston, it takes more than threats of being thrown out the
airlock to make me give up.

(I was so focused on getting to Earth that I completely
forgot about a gift until I was standing in front of Jack
and Marie's apartment door. It was too late, of course—
the door had already scanned my face and announced me.
For a moment, I hoped no one was home but then the
door swung open and my sister-in-law stood framed in
the doorway like a goddess in a painting. The three of us
spent hours talking, then had dinner together, then talked
for a few more hours. It turns out my brother isn't nearly
as insufferable when he's around Marie. Not that I forgot

about my original purpose in visiting them. Before I left, I pulled Jack aside and made him an offer I thought he couldn't refuse. He should take a break from scribbling vague poetry, I said, and write up the story of my life instead. "I already have the whole thing mapped out in my mind in outline," I said, "so all you have to do is flesh it out a little." Who wouldn't want to read my life's story? And his job was about three-quarters done! "I'm living, breathing, pure profit," I said, and offered that he keep a generous percentage of the gain, which even at twenty or (if he plays hardball) twenty-two percent would be an ever-giving wedding gift to him and Marie. Not a writer in a million would turn down such an offer—yet Jack did! Of course I wasn't surprised; but Marie is pregnant so I'll be back once the baby is born and will have another chance to convince Jack of his folly. Like I said, I'm not surprised or daunted. The Good Book did warn me about this—a profit is welcome everywhere except at home.)

T HAT was bad, sir. (*Thank you, old friend. It's a habit I can't shake, ending these logs with a pun. If this is ever formally recognized as a condition, I hope they name it after me. "I've got the JK," people will say, but they'll be just kidding.*) Where are you now? Are you coming back?

(*While traveling to Earth, my first order of business was to complete your promotion paperwork. As I described your skills and abilities, though, I became convinced of something I already suspected, that it would be a waste to send you off to some small commission. This I made clear to the Board: the DeVille deserves a captain like you. And when I was being honest with myself, I knew that there were some things I had to do that I couldn't do as the captain of a warship, responsible for a large military crew. So, no, my friend, I'm not coming back; my retirement is effective in a few weeks. You can pick up the shuttle next time you're near Earth; I've left it with the Board for some repairs (don't worry, it's nothing serious; the last captain whose ship's services I borrowed tried to teach me a lesson as I made my graceful exit, but thankfully his aim was as poor as his manners.)*

(Now, you may know that it's traditional for Board senior officers to provide a formal suggestion in their retirement letters. I'd had my suggestion ready for years (institute mandatory Captain Courageous and the Women Who Love Him *marathon nights, on all ships and on a weekly basis, to boost morale), but hiding in the shuttle in some ship's cargo hold, sitting on the floor, in the dark so the power consumption wouldn't alert security, and scratching away on my touchpad, I changed my mind. My suggestion was to institute mandatory chapels instead, and a chaplain, in each warship in the fleet. People need sacred space, Winston; space that will help them remember that they are people, not just soldiers and officers; space where they can worship together as a community; space where they can feel free to ask questions that aren't normally asked. If you've ever read Other Side propaganda, you'll know that they think of us as Godless, soulless, opportunistic, violent, and without conscience or remorse. Sure* we are, *but they've only ever met Board officers and delegates and those ignoramuses figure that all of humanity is like that! Who knows but that a few chaplains distributed throughout the fleet may help us all reclaim our spiritual side and maybe contribute to a reawakening of*

our dormant consciences, and maybe show the Other Side a different side to us, if you know what I mean.

(*Of course the suggestion will go nowhere, but I had another reason for asking that a chapel be placed on every ship that flies through the galaxy. Can you guess what it is?*)

I THINK I can, sir. Is it to turn warships into birds of pray?

(*Winston, I'm speechless.*)

(*OK, I'm back. Winston, I tell you about an important initiative that could save thousands and maybe millions of souls and lives, perhaps end an interstellar war that has been raging since before either of us was born, and all you can do is make a bad pun?*

(*I've never been prouder.*

(*It turns out the Board has decided to implement my suggestion, though. The cost of war has been high, and the Dr. Evan lookalike spy we sent to the Other Side has reported back: they're not feeling it nearly as much as we are. The chapels and chaplains will be façades to warm the Other Side to us and lay the groundwork for a possible peace treaty. They're doing it in the wrong way and for all the wrong reasons, of course, but God has a way of conquering entire lands once given a single beachhead. If He can work through puns to win someone like me over, imagine what He can do with even fake chapels and chaplains.*

(*They were so happy with the suggestion that I've been called out of retirement and given an admiralty. But the title matters less to me than what I can do with the power. My first mission as admiral, for example, is to lead a del-*

*egation to the coordinates Baby Lon gave us. We're trav-
eling aboard the newly re-commissioned* Ilovelord, *and
carrying with us a cargo hold full of art, books, music,
and movies we want to share with them (and no, Winston,
I'm not bringing the full* Captain Courageous *series with
me. Just the first season. You have to leave them wanting
for more!)*

G OOD for you, Admiral! (*Don't be so formal, Winston,
call me "Sir."*) Thank you for everything (*welcome*)
and good luck (*we spacefarers say "Godspeed," Winston.*)
But is it okay if we communicate through regular channels
now instead of using my personal logs? (*Sure we can.*)

U H, sir? You're not going to try to end on a pun?
(*I'm an admiral now, Winston, and on an important
mission of diplomacy and cultural exchange. Do you really think I have time to think up silly jokes? Maybe you
expect me to remind you that we sent the Dr. Evan lookalike into Other Side space but didn't want to splurge on
Other Side authentic fabric, so that in fact we sent him as
a wolf in cheap clothing, but the joke is not in the wolf in
cheap clothing; or maybe you expect me to construct some
elaborate story about how the Plow family of furniture
makers is capitalizing on the fact that the war is becoming a sore point for the cash-strapped Board by buying
up and converting war factories at bargain prices, effec-
tively turning sores into Plow chairs, but the joke is not
in the sores nor is it in the Plow chairs. No, my friend,
the real joke is a small joke, a divine little paradox. This
joyful joke is that we have a God who is willing to conde-
scend and reach out to us any way He can, a God who will
meet us on our level and speak to us face-to-face, whether*

through jokes, or in a burning bush that somehow isn't burned up, or, most marvelously, as a Baby kicking His feet and giggling, a Baby like any another except that He also happens to be the Creator of the universe.

(Tell me, Winston, what joke could I make that would be more delightful than that celestial one, which has filled the hearts of billions of people with hope and joy for thousands of years? Of course I want to end this here and now, so that you'd have every reason to whisper an assenting word of worship and praise, rather than try to cap this off with a silly pun, which will only lead you, instead, to groan out an exasperated "Ah man.")

About the Author

KARL EL-KOURA was born in Dubai, United Arab Emirates in 1979 and currently lives in Canada's capital city with his beautiful editor-wife. He has published more than sixty short stories and articles. Karl holds a second-degree black belt in Okinawan Goju Ryu karate, is an avid commuter-cyclist, and works for the Canadian Federal Public Service.

Karl maintains an online home at www.ootersplace.com, where you can discover more work by him and keep up-to-date with his latest news. He can be reached at karl@ootersplace.com.

Also by the Author

Ooter's Place and Other Stories of Faith, Fear, and Love

Why doesn't God do something to stop the evil and suffering in the world? Some people who call themselves the "Atheists Against God" think they know the answer. And they know what they're going to do about it, too.

A hired gun—who doesn't use a gun and won't be hired by just anyone—realizes that his profession is killing him, but finds it hard to quit. Until he discovers that his talent has more uses than he ever dreamed possible.

A young boy learns that his best friend is an alien. But does that mean they have to stop being friends?

Meet interesting, complex characters; explore worlds both strange and all-too-familiar; and discover the answer to thought-provoking mysteries in this collection of 13 short stories by Karl El-Koura. Twelve of these short tales were previously published in magazines between 1998 and 2010, while the bonus story is exclusive to this collection.

Spanning a wide range of genres (including science fiction, fantasy, horror, detective fiction, military fiction, and superhero fiction) and a wide range of lengths (from the shortest story at 250 words to the longest at 7500 words), *Ooter's Place and Other Stories of Fear, Faith, and Love* is an eclectic collection. Join the author as he introduces you to stories both light and dark, fun and serious, always entertaining.

Visit www.ootersplace.com/OotersPlace
for more information.